Zoë
and the Fairy Crown

For Jeremy

First published in Great Britain in 2001
by Piccadilly Press Ltd.,
5 Castle Road, London NW1 8PR

Designed by Louise Millar
Printed and bound in Belgium by Proost

ISBN: 1 85340 649 X (hardback)
1 85340 644 9 (paperback)

3 5 7 9 10 8 6 4 2

A catalogue record of this book
is available from the British Library

Jane Andrews has two sons and lives in Redhill in Surrey.
Since graduating from art college she has undertaken a variety
of graphic work, including illustrations for magazines.
Piccadilly Press also publish the other books in this series,
Zoë at Fairy School and **Zoë the Tooth Fairy**:

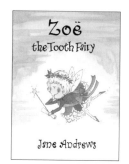

ISBN: 1 85340 640 6 (p/b)   ISBN: 1 85340 651 1 (p/b)

Zoë
and the Fairy Crown

Jane Andrews

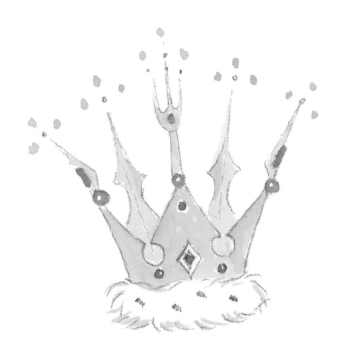

Piccadilly Press • London

It was the Fairy Queen's birthday. There was going to be
a special party. Zoë and Pip flew to the castle clutching
their presents. They were bubbling with excitement.

The Fairy Queen was in her dressing-room putting on her best party crown. She was delighted with Zoë's and Pip's presents.

"This will be the best party ever!" said the Fairy Queen.
"The elves are doing a big barbecue this evening.
Everyone is invited."

All the fairies had a wonderful time at the party.
There was a competition for formation wand waving,
and one for balancing skills. Some fairies did a special
magic display. Others tried trampolining.

What a surprise!
The Fairy Queen was bouncing on the trampoline.
She bounced higher and higher and higher.
Then suddenly . . .

. . . the Fairy Queen's crown
flew off her head and into
the sky like a rocket!

"Oh, no!" cried the Fairy Queen. "My party crown!"
"Don't worry," said Zoë. "We'll find it."
The fairies looked everywhere – behind rocks, under toadstools, even in the stream. They searched and searched until it started to get dark. But the crown had disappeared.

Just as the sun was setting Zoë had a brilliant idea. "We can make light beams with our wings and keep on looking!" Zoë and Pip showed all the fairies how to flutter their wings in just the right way.

In the forest, the elves were
building a big fire for the barbecue.
Suddenly a small elf spotted something very shiny and spiky
in a tree. "This is perfect for roasting marshmallows!" he cried.

All the elves gathered round the blazing bonfire.
The fairies flew in to join them.
"Sorry we are late," said Zoë. "We've been looking for the
Fairy Queen's crown. It's lost and the Fairy Queen is very sad."
"Cheer up and have something to eat," said the small elf,
lowering something bright and shiny over the fire.
"Marshmallow, anyone?"

Zoë and Pip gasped.

It was the Fairy Queen's crown!
"Stop!" cried Zoë to the elf. But he couldn't hear
over the crackle of the fire.
"Quick," cried Pip. "We must rescue it!"
But the fire was too hot, and the two little fairies
nearly burned their wings.

"We must use our magic wands," said Zoë.
"It's the only way."
Together Pip and Zoë waved their wands at the crown.
"I hope this will work," thought Zoë to herself.
There was a great whoosh and a swirl of sparkles . . .

. . . and the crown fell gently into Zoë's hands, all covered
in marshmallows.

"Oh, Zoë and Pip, how clever!" cried the Fairy Queen.
"This is the best birthday present of all!"